Have You
Seen Mary?

Written by Jeff Kurrus
Photographs by Michael Forsberg

For LH and MK – JK
For EF and EF – MF

Have You Seen Mary?
Written by Jeff Kurrus
Photographs by Michael Forsberg
ISBN 978-0-9916389-0-1

R.R. Donnelley & Sons Company
Printed in Mexico
April, 2014
2nd Printing

Book design by Reigert Graphics, Lincoln, Nebraska

Visit www.haveyouseenmary.com

Introduction

Dear Readers,

Before you read Jeff Kurrus's *Have You Seen Mary?*, one question must be asked: what parts of this fictional story are real?

Well, many parts are, starting with where Nebraska's visiting sandhill cranes come from. They spend their winters in northern Mexico and southern United States in places like Bosque del Apache National Wildlife Refuge in New Mexico. Then, during their spring migration, more than five hundred thousand cranes traveling north through what is known as the Central Flyway stop along the Platte River in Nebraska, making this the largest gathering of cranes in the world.

While in the Platte River Valley, they eat corn left over from last fall's harvest for much needed energy. But like us, they need a balanced diet. They also forage for insects, snails, worms, mice, snakes, frogs and other plant material before eventually flying on to their nesting grounds in Canada, Alaska, and Siberia, sometimes covering five hundred miles a day.

Besides food, cranes stop at the Platte River in Nebraska because it is wide and shallow. Because they cannot roost, or sleep, in trees, cranes spend their nights in the cold, shallow river, away from predators like coyotes. Other predators include fox, bobcats, mountain lions, eagles, just to name a few. A crane's life, especially during migration, is never easy.

Cranes are also like us in many ways. Colts, or young cranes, in the same family fight with each other just like we do if we have brothers or sisters. Plus, crane families will also quarrel with other families. Cranes start their own families by dating, and will stay with one mate for a long time, often their entire lives. They live around twenty years, but there are scattered reports of wild cranes living into their thirties. As they age, they turn from a light brown color when they are young to gray as they grow up and even go bald.

Cranes also take baths and preen, or groom, their feathers. They wear a type of make-up, smearing reddish-colored mud on their gray feathers. One reason they do this is for camouflage. Another is to remove pests from their skin and feathers. Others believe they do it to pretty themselves for their mate. Plus, their voices even change as they grow up, which brings me to one more question: do cranes really talk?

Yes they do. Cranes look alike, but they have different sounding voices. They also have many different calls they use. One is the contact call. That is one of the calls that this story's characters, John and Mary, would use in real life to find each other. Cranes also use body language and even the red patch, which is actually skin, to communicate. Think how you tell others how you are feeling just by the way you hold your body or use your eyebrows. Cranes are doing the same thing.

By reading this story, I hope you'll see that sandhill cranes are, in many ways, just like us. But what I really hope is that this book makes you want to learn even more about these fascinating animals.

— *Keanna Leonard*
Education Director of Iain Nicolson Audubon Center at Rowe Sanctuary, Nebraska

When John and Mary Crane finally cupped their wings toward the Platte River in Nebraska after flying more than six hundred miles from New Mexico, the same excitement that filled them each year was back again.

For them, this river brought
back so many memories –
from watching their chicks
grow up and start their own
families ...

... to admiring the wide open sunsets
that only Nebraska could offer.

However, this year was different than most. With no young of their own, all of their time would be dedicated to building strength for the last leg of their flight to their breeding grounds in Alaska.

Corn, snails, earthworms, and water – oh yes, sweet Platte River water – would add the energy needed for their journey home.

They drank when they landed, each swallow filling every inch of their tired bodies.

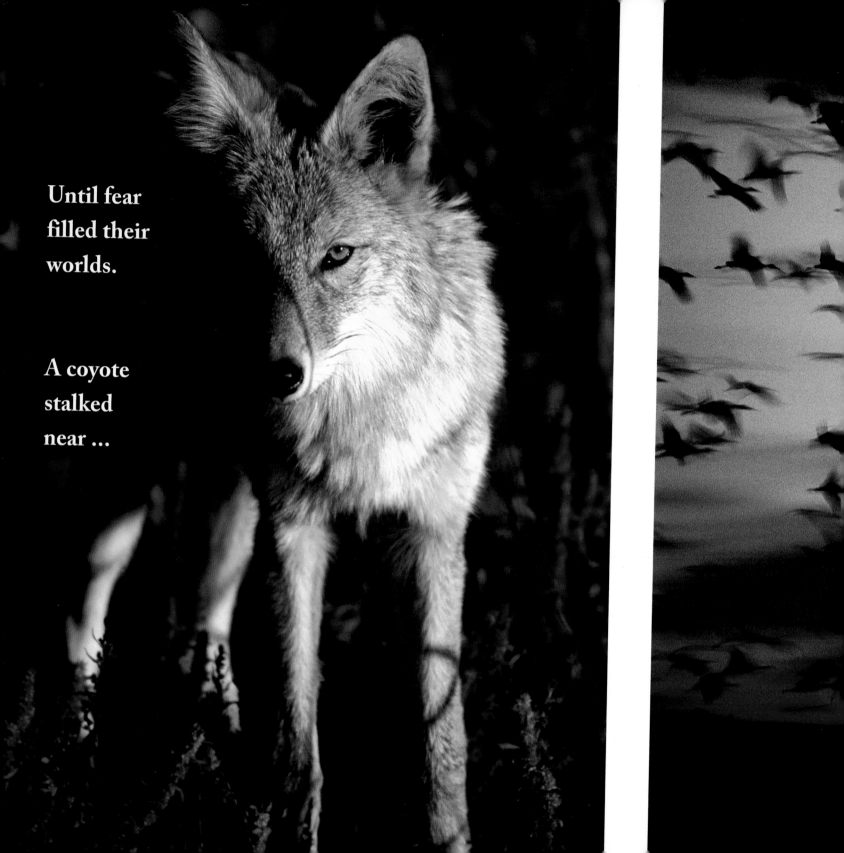

Until fear
filled their
worlds.

A coyote
stalked
near ...

... and the sky blackened with dark, gray bodies.

In the blurry confusion, John lost Mary.

When John
landed back
onto one of the
many sandbars
along the river,
he did not
search for her.

"We will
meet again
tomorrow,"
he thought,
tucking his
head beneath
his wing to get
some much
needed rest.

13

The following morning, John walked along the cold, shallow river. Everywhere he looked he saw cranes, and crane tracks, but no Mary.

"Are crane feet like snowflakes?" he wondered. He knew her feathers and the sound of her voice, but had no idea what her feet looked like. Why hadn't he paid more attention?

As he searched,
he watched
cranes fight.

And he watched
them bathe.

But not once did he see Mary.

Finally, John approached another crane.

"Excuse me," he said. "Have you seen Mary? She stands about four feet tall, and has the most beautiful gray feathers on all the Platte."

"You're going to have to narrow that down a little," the crane said. "We all look like that."

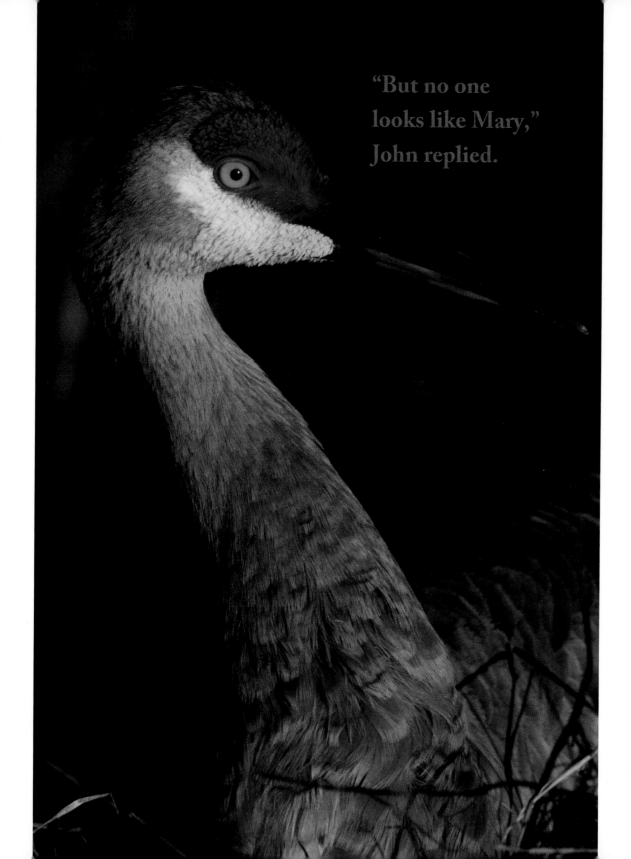

"But no one
looks like Mary,"
John replied.

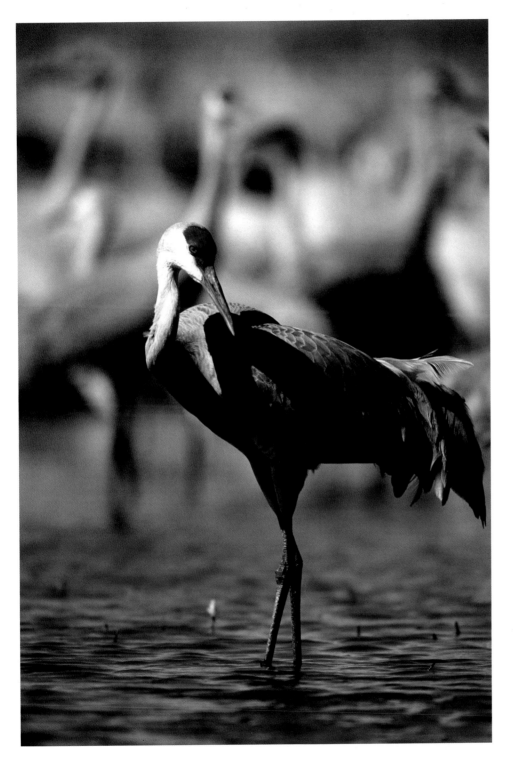

"Just like no one looks like her," the other crane responded with a smile, pointing to his preening soul mate.

John thanked him and continued his lonely walk down the river.

As he explored, he remembered their early summer mornings at Denali National Park in Alaska ...

... and their late winter afternoons at Bosque del Apache National Wildlife Refuge in New Mexico.

John was brought back to the present as flock after flock flew from the river. His heart sank low in his chest, for not once did he hear her voice or see the glow from her feathers.

The cranes would now be separated along the Platte, from the towns of Grand Island to Lexington, in more than eighty miles of fields, creeks, and meadows. It could take him all day to find her. He lifted into the air and continued his search.

23

His first stop was near the town of Wood River. Long ago, Mary had convinced him that the fields there had the tastiest insects on the Plains. He landed near a flock of cranes, more than one hundred birds.

"Excuse me," he asked the group. "Do you know Mary from the Yukon Delta?"

"No," said one crane.
"Not me," said another.
"Uh-uh," said a third,
and the rest just shook their heads.

So then he asked one deer.

Next he asked two ducks.

Finally he asked three whoopers.

But they all said no.

Near sunset, John had a new idea. He would go back to the Platte, where they had first landed the night before, and watch every flight return to roost.

The idea gave him hope, and he quickly flew to the river.

But that hope disappeared as cranes came to roost. When he thought there couldn't possibly be space on the Platte for another bird, a thousand more would land.

"Why didn't we talk about what we would do if we were ever separated?" he asked himself. "Why didn't we have a plan?"

He repeated questions to himself as light disappeared from the day. It was going to be a long night. Because he could not sleep, he guarded a nearby flock, eyes wide and alert.

As he watched the banks for predators, he asked himself more questions.

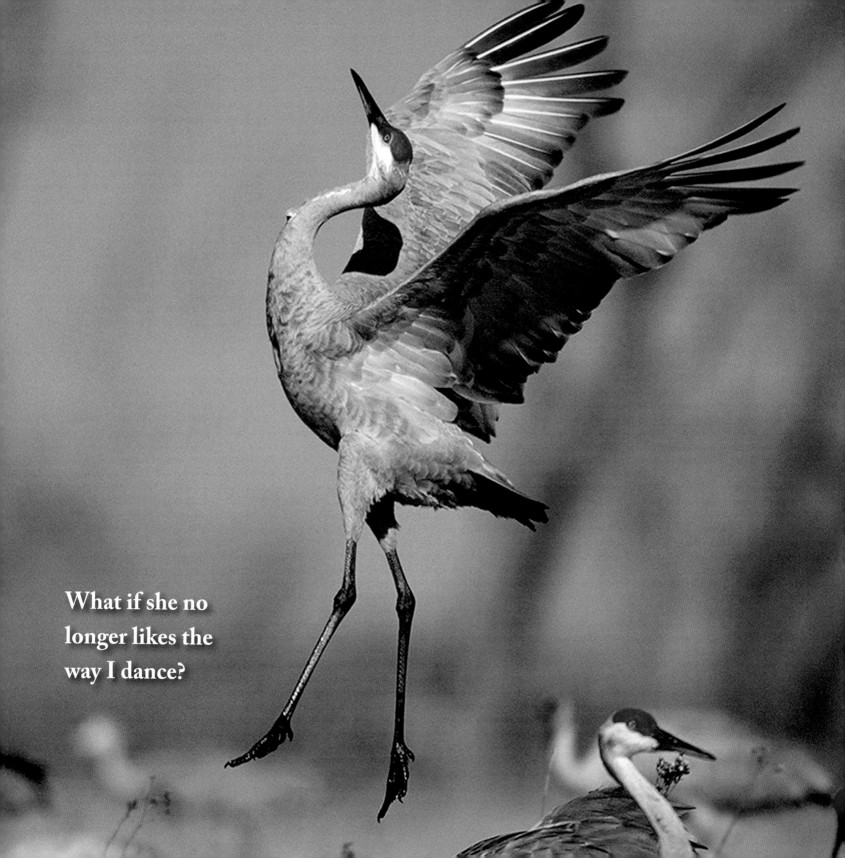

What if she no
longer likes the
way I dance?

Or the way I unison call?

What if she has found someone new?

He closed his eyes and prayed, remembering their
past flights together.

His search continued for nearly a month as he asked countless animals if they knew her.

This is how she flies,
he told the meadowlark.

This is how she paints herself
with mud on the nest, he told the
ornate box turtle.

This is how she sounds
when she's happy, he told
the chorus frog.

And this is how she holds our chicks, he told everyone.

But not one animal
had seen Mary.

By the afternoon of John's thirtieth day, he was weary. He had drunk little and eaten less. He was ten years old, not very old for a sandhill crane, yet he felt twice that. Lost, and more tired than he had ever been, he leaned over for a drink.

There, in a blade of grass by the river's edge, was a lone feather shining brighter than any he had ever seen. "Mary," he spoke. But when he turned to look for her, she wasn't there.

"There is one more place to look," he said, thinking of the spot he had avoided since their arrival – the power lines.

Each year hundreds of birds were killed by flying into power lines crossing the Platte. While large yellow markers were recently added so cranes could see them better, that still didn't keep some birds from flying into them.

John walked hesitantly in their direction.

And despite all the noise around him, the loudest sound was his nervous heart.

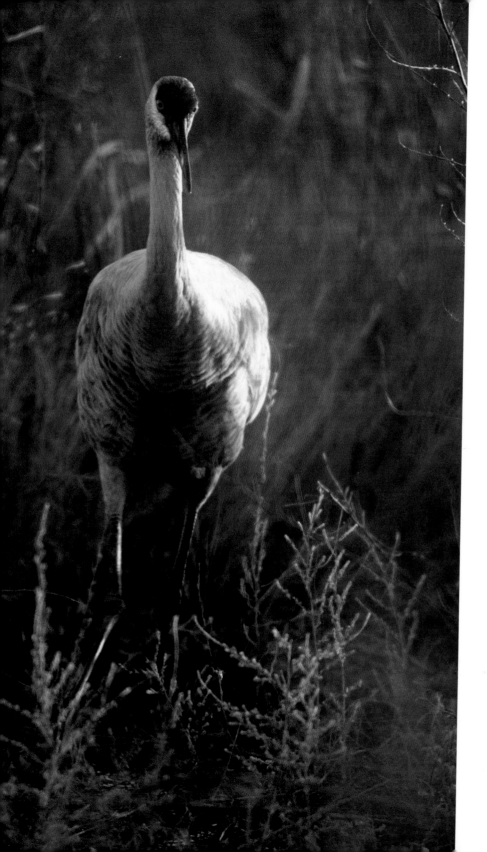

Yet when he arrived at the lines, she was not there. Momentarily relieved, he looked up and saw cranes everywhere. "I may never find her," he thought.

"It looks like someone hasn't been eating," floated a sweet and distinctive voice from behind John, and he knew it was Mary even before he turned.

To the untrained eye, there was no difference. Gray, with a red patch above her eyes, she looked the same as any other crane.

Except she glowed different than all the others.

"I've been looking for you," he said.

"And I for you," Mary replied. "I've been leaving feathers for you."

He leapt as high as he could, staring into her eyes as he did.

"I love it when you do that," she said. "The way you dance, the way you call – I love everything about you."

There was so much to say, so much to share, but all they could do was look at each other. Finally, Mary spoke. "It looks like we'll have a beautiful sunset. And in the morning we have to fatten you up. We have a long trip north soon."

"I don't want to think about flying yet," he said. "I just want to be here, with you."
"Me too," she replied.